THREE TO GET READY

by Betty Boegehold

Pictures by Mary Chalmers

An I CAN READ Book

HARPER & ROW, PUBLISHERS   NEW YORK

FOR KAREN

THREE TO GET READY

Text copyright © 1965 by Betty Doyle Boegehold
Pictures copyright © 1965 by Mary Chalmers

Printed in the United States of America. All rights reserved. No part
of this book may be used or reproduced in any manner whatsoever
without written permission except in the case of brief quotations
embodied in critical articles and reviews. For information address
Harper & Row, Publishers, Incorporated, 49 East 33rd Street,
New York 16, N.Y.

LIBRARY OF CONGRESS CATALOG CARD NUMBER: 62–8042

THREE TO GET READY

This is the story of three kittens,

George,

Ginger,

and Gigi.

And their mother.

Their mother is always there.

GEORGE

George was very sorry.

George was very sorry for George.

He thought,

"Gigi's fish looks better than my fish.

Ginger's fish looks better than my fish.

They have a better supper than I have."

So George bit Gigi,

and   orge scratched Ginger.

Mother Cat washed Gigi's ear.

She washed Ginger's tail.

Then she said to George,

"I think you got up

on the wrong side

of the bed this morning.

You have been cross all day.

Very, very cross.

Now go play by yourself."

George thought,

"I will not play by myself.

I will go away.

I will go away forever.

Then they will be sorry.

They will wish they had

me to play with.

But they won't—not ever."

So away went George forever.

He went out the door,

out into the world.

It was dark out in the world.

The world in the night did not look

like the world in the day.

There were dark things all around.

Funny little bugs made bits of light

in the dark.

George ran after one.

He jumped at another.

The bugs flew away,

but the dark things didn't.

They were still all around.

George couldn't see his house,

his warm, bright house

with milk and fish and Mother.

He began to cry.

Then someone said, "Now, now!"

Mother Cat was there.

He put his nose in her warm fur.

He smelled the warm, sweet fur

as she washed him all over

with a soft, sandpaper washing.

And he saw that the dark things

all around were only trees

and sticks and stones.

"Such a silly black kitten,"

said Mother Cat

as they went back home.

"We like three kittens," she said

as they crossed the floor.

"We need three kittens," she said

as George pushed

between Ginger and Gigi.

"Always?" asked George sleepily.

"Always," said his mother.

"Now do get up

on the right side

of the bed tomorrow."

GIGI

Gigi, Ginger, and George

were three months old.

So they had a birthday,

a three-months-old birthday.

They wore birthday bows—

yellow, blue, and red.

They washed themselves all over.

They were birthday clean.

They all had birthday presents.

A red ball for George,

a blue ball for Ginger,

and a yellow ball for Gigi.

Ginger bit the blue ball hard.

He wanted to see what was in it.

Gigi batted her yellow ball

back and forth.

But George bounced
the red ball hard.
So hard,
it went under a chair
and rolled out
near Gigi.

Gigi put one paw
on the red ball
and one paw
on the yellow ball.
"Now I have two,"
she said.

"Give me back my ball," said George.

Gigi sat on the red ball and said,

"Finders keepers, losers weepers."

"Bad Gigi," cried Ginger.

"Give George back his red ball."

"It is my ball now," said Gigi.

"Now I have two."

19

"Gigi is a bad, bad cat!

Come play with my blue ball,"

said Ginger to George.

"We will have a ball game."

They batted the blue ball all around.

Pounce! Bat!

Gigi couldn't play with two balls.

She had to sit on the red ball

and hold the yellow ball with her paws.

"I don't care," said Gigi.

"Finders keepers, losers weepers."

"Happy birthday to you,

happy birthday to you,"

sang Mother Cat.

There was a lovely cake.

A cat birthday cake

with three little candles.

It was a lovely fish cake

with a lovely fish smell.

"Now blow hard," said Mother.

George blew so hard,

Ginger blew such a big puff,

that the candles went out.

Gigi couldn't blow.

She couldn't eat the birthday cake.

She could only smell

the lovely fishy smell.

Gigi had to sit on the red ball

and hold the yellow ball.

"I have two balls," she said.

"Two for me.

Who wants an old fish cake anyhow?"

"All the more for us,"

said Ginger and George.

They ate up every fishy bit.

Mother just looked at Gigi.

"Finders keepers, losers weepers,"

said Gigi.

Then George and Ginger

began to be sleepy.

They had played so much

and eaten so much,

they were tired.

They lay close to Mother Cat.

She sang a happy-birthday song

in a sleepy, soft purr.

Gigi was tired too.

She was tired of sitting on the red ball
and holding the yellow ball.

She was tired of not playing.

She was tired of being alone.

She began to cry.

"I don't want your red ball,"
she said to George.
"Here is your red ball
and my yellow ball too.
I don't want them now."

Mother said softly,

"Sometimes finders are weepers."

She opened her green eyes

and purred a deep purr.

"Come, my calico kitten,

between my fur paws.

Come close and lie still

between my fur paws.

Sleep away, my little cats.

Tomorrow is another day

to play another way."

GINGER

"Stay in the yard.

Stay in the yard to play,"

said Mother Cat.

"Outside the yard

is the world.

We will go out

in the world together.

But not today."

Then Mother went away

on Mother-Cat business.

Gigi and George began to play.

But Ginger did not.

Ginger thought,

"Why can't I

just look at the world?

Just a little look?

I'm a big cat now.

I know all about the yard.

So I will just peek

at the world."

Ginger put his tail up

and marched across the grass.

He marched right up to the gate.

He put his nose under the gate

and took a little peek at the world.

The world looked just like the yard.

Just grass and trees and a wind blowing.

"Well," thought Ginger.

"Maybe the world

will not be the same as the yard

if I walk out in it a little way.

Just a little walk into the world."

Ginger pushed himself under the gate
and walked out into the world.

The grass was green and hot.

The trees were tall.

And the wind blew in his fur.

"Just like the yard," thought Ginger.

Then Ginger heard a new noise.

Ginger saw something new.

A big brown dog

making a big-dog noise

was bouncing across the grass

right at Ginger.

So up a tree went Ginger.

Way, way up.

The big brown dog sat under the tree

and looked at him.

Ginger held tight to the tree
with all his kitten claws
and looked at the dog.
Ginger wished and wished he were
home safely with Gigi and George.
He wished and wished he were home.

After a while the dog went away,

and there was Ginger

alone in the tree.

He did not know how to get down.

He held on tight

and called for Mother

with a thin, kitten cry.

"Here I am," said Mother Cat.

And she was there.

Right at the bottom of the tree.

"Come down, my Ginger boy.

And we will go home together,"

said Mother.

But Ginger could not go down.

He didn't know how!

"Just put one paw down
and then another,"

his mother said.

"One paw after another

will take you home."

Ginger began to come down.

One paw at a time.

One step and then another,

until he was close to Mother.

They went back under the gate together.

Gigi and George were in the yard

pouncing and playing.

"I don't like the world," said Ginger.

"I will never go out

of the yard again. Not ever!"

Mother Cat began to wash him.

She purred and washed his face.

"There is a time for the yard

and a time for the world.

Now it is time for play."

THREE KITTENS AND MOTHER

"Come along, my dears,"

said Mother Cat.

"Now it is time to see the world

for a little while."

46

Ginger and George, Gigi and Mother,
went out of the gate
and up the hill
to see the world.

"The world is full of noise,"

said Ginger.

"I will see what that noise is."

Whirr, went something in the grass.

Ginger put his nose in the grass.

Out jumped a grasshopper!

Click, click, went something

under a stone.

Ginger batted the stone

with his paw.

Out popped a clicking bug!

Buzz, *buzz*, went something in a flower.

Ginger put his nose in the flower.

Out flew a buzzing bee!

"Oh, my poor nose," cried Ginger.

"The world does not stay still,"

said Gigi. "I will stop it."

Pounce! went Gigi on a blowing leaf.

Pounce! went Gigi on the bending grass.

Pounce! went Gigi on a waving tail.

"Oh, my poor, dear tail," cried Gigi.

"The world is big," said George.

"But I am big too.

I can catch this ant."

Pounce!

"I can catch that beetle."

Jump!

"I can catch this little green string."

Hop!

But the little green string

went away fast

with a zig-zag into the grass.

George went away fast too.

"Mother, wait for me!" cried George.

Then they came to the top of the world,

Ginger and George,

Gigi and Mother.

There was the world all around them.

The warm-yellow, green-cool world
full of cat things to play with.
Pounce! Jump! Bite! Play!
Their mother watched them,
purring a happy-cat purr.

"The world is big," said George.

"It's a warm and windy world,"
cried Gigi.

"It's a green world
full of things for a cat to catch,"
said Ginger.

"This is a cat world, a pounce world,

a world of purr and play,"

sang Ginger and George

and Gigi.

"The world is too big

and too full of things

for a cat to catch in a day,"

said their mother.

"Now come along home."

So down the hill they went.

Ginger, Gigi, and George.

Pounce! Jump! Run! Play!

While their mother

walked close behind.